# Esth Bunny

Written and Illustrated by
## Keri K. Thompson

Creachy Peach
PUBLISHING

Copyright ©2021 by Keri K. Thompson

All rights reserved. No part of this book may be reproduced or used in any manner without written permission of the copyright owner except for use of quotations in a book review.

ISBN 978-1-7358839-1-5

Published by Creachy Peach Publishing

For Mama and Daddy, who have always shown me what sacrificial love truly means.

For Ben, who believes in me and supports me unconditionally.

When winter's nap is over,
And the sun warms up the earth,
Each day brings new life blooming,
Spring is the season of rebirth.

A little rabbit went exploring,
For some clover to nibble on.
Her name was Esther Bunny,
And her journey had just begun.

As she foraged in the cool grass,
Not one clover did she find.
But something else caught her eye,
A treasure of a different kind.

On a dry riverbed, not very far,
Revealed by the sun ray's light,
As Esther peered through the blades,
It gleamed from its surface of white.

She approached it with caution,
For she was quite unaware,
The discovery she had made,
Would be an answered prayer.

Esther had been questioning,
Although she was quite content,
Lately she had been wondering,
What her purpose in life meant.

Was there more to it than this,
Simply spending out her days,
Searching through the weeds,
For something new to graze?

The very thing she sought after,
Although she did not yet realize,
Was the very thing she had found,
In a lonesome egg, it was disguised.

She felt her instincts tingling,
It was instantly ever so clear.
She knew she had to protect it,
By keeping the egg very near.

But she felt wetness on her nose,
As big raindrops began to fall,
And it was suddenly quite evident,
That this place was not safe at all.

She scooped her egg up in her paws,
So from the danger she could flee,
But the riverbed that once was dry,
became a rushing stream so swiftly.

As Esther gripped her new egg friend,
And the water rushed all around her,
She caught hold of the arms of a root,
So she could escape from the water.

Esther, exhausted from the battle,
Smiled down at the egg where it fell,
But her relief soon turned to grief,
When she saw the small crack on its shell.

She gathered her precious cargo,
To trek up higher on the hillside,
For she knew for the egg's protection,
It would be a safer place to abide.

But a fleeting shadow fell across,
The path on which they journeyed,
And Esther knew without a doubt,
They must find shelter in a hurry.

A hawk was flying over her head,
He was searching for his prey,
And Esther worried for her egg,
So for guidance she did pray.

And there up on the hilltop crest,
Her answer, revealed so clearly.
She hopped as fast as she knew how,
To the shelter of a dogwood tree.

The daylight's end was drawing near,
As the sky turned violet, then indigo.
And Esther curled up beside the egg,
To rest under the moonlight's glow.

But danger slithered on the ground,
Too close to the friends' place of rest,
As a snake was looking for a snack,
And an egg would please him best.

When the sound of hissing drew near,
It caused Esther to startle awake.
As he went to strike, Esther laid on the egg,
And kicked her feet hard at the snake.

Defeated, the serpent retreated,
But Esther had been made aware,
She must build a nest around the egg,
That would make predators beware.

She scurried into the shrubs and brush,
For the twigs to build her masterpiece,
And when her labor of love was completed,
She knew her egg would find some peace.
For the protective bed she had designed,
Was a harshly pointed and thorny place.

While she moved the egg into the nest,
She noticed more cracks on its surface.
So she laid on top, although it caused pain,
For protecting the egg was her purpose.

Esther, not long drifted off, was awoken,
By the sound of men's voices approaching.
So she gathered her egg and fled to a bush,
Where she witnessed the men encroaching.

She watched them, in helpless horror,
As her shielding tree they cut down,
And one of the men muttered something,
As he put the nest on like a crown.

As quick as they came into her safe harbor,
They left, taking with them her hope.
She felt defeated, lost and alone.
She did not know how she could cope.

She looked down at her pure white egg,
Now with too may cracks to count.
And she examined her own furry coat,
Taking her many wounds into account.

On a hill far away, Esther was unaware,
That the scars and bruises she'd worn,
Would also belong to One who would wear,
Her loving nest as a crown of thorns,

And the tree that, once used for shelter,
Bore witness to her sacrifice from above,
Would become a cross for One other,
Yet it would remain a shelter of love.

From where Esther sat with her egg,
She felt the ground as it trembled.
As the earth quaked beneath her feet,
What hope she had left dissembled.

To keep the egg from rolling away,
One by one, she placed each stone,
Until she had built a nest of pebbles,
Covered the egg, then left it alone.

As she slowly hopped down the hill,
She collapsed under her burden.
For she had not fulfilled her calling,
And her bunny heart was hurting.

Three times the sun did set and rise,
As the woeful rabbit lay in mourning,
But hope arose with the dawn's light,
On Esther bunny's Easter morning.

A single stone had been rolled away,
And down the hillside it bounded,
Striking Esther on its journey down,
Leaving her puzzled and astounded.

She hurried to the tomb she had built,
But what she found was not her friend.
Instead, an empty shell in many pieces,
And she wondered what had happened.

And then, she felt a strange feeling,
A peaceful presence shown from above.
She turned to see her once egg friend,
Had now become a pure white dove.

The friends embraced one another,
And Esther realized that day,
That what she had been protecting,
Was indeed her saving grace.

As she watched the dove fly upward,
Esther bunny would always know,
That through pure hope and sacrifice,
The greatest love will grow.

"This is love: not that we loved God, but that he loved us and sent his Son as an atoning sacrifice for our sins."

1 John 4:10

Made in the USA
Columbia, SC
26 March 2021